WARNING!
THIS BOOK MAY CONTAIN RABBITS!

tim warnes

LITTLE TIGER PRESS
London

coracle

lily

lily pad

Mole loved labelling things.

All sorts of things.

Anything really.

It was his absolute top thing to do.

His best friend, the Lumpy-Bumpy Thing, was rather good at it too.

One day, the two friends
spotted something unusual
on the path.

"**Look!**" gasped Mole. "A **snow bunny!**
I've seen **brown** bunnies and **black** bunnies
and **grey** bunnies before, but I've never seen
a white one."

It was very mysterious indeed.

Mole started to
label the bunny.
But it bounced
away.

"Stop that bunny!"
cried Mole.

So the Lumpy-Bumpy Thing
chased after it.

The Lumpy-Bumpy Thing came back
wearing an interesting-looking hat.

The hat already had a label:

WARNING! Do not touch!

"Quick! Take it off!"
cried Mole. "It could be dangerous."

But the Lumpy-Bumpy Thing just giggled. Then it lifted up the hat.

There, on its head, was another bunny, with a very tickly tail.

"Holey moley!" gasped Mole. "That hat's magic!"

The bunny jumped down
and gave Mole
a great, big snuggle.
"I suppose it's
safe enough," Mole
grinned. "After all,
they ARE just bunnies."

On-off, on-off went the magic hat.
"Look how many bunnies you've made!"
exclaimed Mole. "I'm going to number them so we
can play Bunny Bingo!"

The Lumpy-Bumpy Thing was in Bunny Heaven!

But Mole was not. Those **naughty** bunnies kept swapping places and muddling themselves up.

It was all **very confusing**.

"Ten, seven, nine, five – **wait!** That's **not right**,"
grumbled Mole. **"Keep still!"**
But the bunnies wouldn't listen.

Bunny after bunny
jumped out from the hat.

"97, 98, 99, 100!"

What had started out
as a Bit Of Fun quickly
became a Bit
Of A Problem.

"Make it STOP!" hollered Mole.

The Lumpy-Bumpy Thing tried pushing the bunnies back in the hat. But they were too wriggly.

It tried scaring them away. But they weren't bothered at all.

"Look at this mess!" wailed Mole.
 The bunnies had eaten all the flower
 They'd dug hundreds of holes.
 And now they were pooping all
over the place!

"Stop it!
Bad bunnies!"
cried mole.

Then the Lumpy-Bumpy Thing spotted Something Terrible! Number 54 was heading straight for Mole's vegetable patch . . .

Mole ran after him.
"Give me that carrot!"
he demanded.

They **tugged** and they **pulled**,

and they **pulled** and they **tugged**, until . . .

DOING!

Number 54 let go.

"Ha ha! Got it!" shouted Mole, waving the carrot triumphantly in the air. The other bunnies stopped and stared and twitched their noses . . .

... then they **CHARGED!**

"RUN FOR IT!"
yelled Mole.

But the Lumpy-Bumpy Thing stumbled.
Mole's carrot sailed through the air . . .

. . . and fell with a **plop!** into the magic hat.

One of the bunnies dived in after it . . . and disappeared!

"Hooray!" cried Mole. "Quick! Grab some more carrots!"

So the two friends started hurling them into the hat. And one by one, the bunnies followed.

"Ten, nine, eight, seven, six, five, four, three, two, one, ZERO BUNNIES!" declared Mole. "We did it!"

The Lumpy-Bumpy Thing
peered nervously
into the hat.

"Don't worry," said Mole.
"They've gone now."

Very carefully they
carried it back to
where they'd found it.

"We don't want any more trouble, do we?" said Mole.

But the Lumpy-Bumpy Thing was looking at something unusual in the grass – something with a label on it.

"Don't touch that!" gulped Mole.

But it was too late . . .

"Holey moley!" cried Mole.
"Not again!"